MW01599274

To Ed & Sheila,

Buried Talents

An Inspirational Novella

By Shari Broyer

Blessings!

Shari Broyer

Rights and Disclaimers

This novella is a work of fiction. Any references to real people, events, establishments, organizations, or locales are intended only to provide a sense of authenticity, and are used fictitiously. All other characters, and all incidents and dialogue, are drawn from the author's imagination and are not to be construed as real.

Also by the Author

Jesus on a Park Bench
This Amazon bestselling inspirational short story is striking a chord with readers, remaining in the top 100 in its category over a year after its release on 12-24-12, available on Amazon in Kindle and paperback formats:
http://www.amazon.com/Jesus-Park-Bench-ebook/dp/B00ASS4G2M/ref=sr_1_3?s=books&ie=U
TF8&qid=1356484310&sr=1-
3&keywords=Shari+Broyer

The Neighbors
A short inspirational story, available on Kindle:
http://www.amazon.com/The-Neighbors-ebook/dp/B00BS10QM2/ref=sr_1_5?s=digital-text&ie=UTF8&qid=1363068367&sr=1-
5&keywords=the+neighbors

Petty Theft
A fun, family-friendly mystery, available on Kindle:
http://www.amazon.com/Petty-Theft-ebook/dp/B008P1HW2A/ref=sr_1_1?s=digital-text&ie=UTF8&qid=1343332107&sr=1-
1&keywords=Petty+Theft#_

Table of Contents

Listen

Listen to your inner voice —
The one that's deep inside,
That quiet, strong voice,
The one that will not be denied.

That voice is God within you,
His light just waiting to shine,
For you are God's creation,
A part of the Divine.

God created you for a purpose,
And tucked it safely within your heart.
It is the one thing that feels right for you,
From which you never can depart.

No matter how widely you detour
From the path He has chosen for you,
He will bring you back time and again,
He knows what is yours to do.

And it is only in fulfilling your purpose
That you will truly rejoice,
You will be happy and feel loved
ONLY when you listen to His voice.

Shari Broyer
©August 12, 1999

Chapter 1

"Sara! Where's my green jacket?" Geoff bellowed up the stairs.

"It's hanging in the hall closet with the other coats," Sara—who was busy trying to remove the gum her daughter had gotten into her long blonde hair—replied.

"Ouch, Mom! Do you have to pull so hard?" Abby complained, swatting at her mother's hands.

"Sorry, honey. It's kind of hard to work this peanut butter through the mess."

"I think it's gross that you're putting peanut butter in my hair. It really will be a mess when you get done with it," Abby grimaced.

It wouldn't have been a mess at all if you'd listened to me and spat your gum out before you got into bed last night, Sara thought but didn't say aloud.

She knew from hard experience that her fourteen-year-old daughter, who was on the wild hormonal cusp of womanhood and was also too much like her belligerent father, would only argue against her until she won, even if it was only by default because she was too worn down to defend herself any longer.

"My green jacket's not down here, Sara! What the heck did you do with it?" came the second volley up the stairs.

"Sit tight," Sara said to Abby, who was perched on the closed lid of toilet seat in the upstairs bathroom. "I'll be right back."

Sara went to the master bedroom and entered the walk-in closet. She rifled through all the clothing on Geoff's side. No green jacket. Navigating downstairs, she approached the coat closet in the hall just off the main foyer where her husband stood, hands on hips, a frown marring the face that she had once thought the most handsome she'd ever laid eyes on. She supposed others still found it so, especially those women she was forced to watch him flirt with at company dinners, but then, they had never seen his countenance the way she did on a daily basis—all red and mottled with anger. Now Geoff gave her a dirty look and tapped his foot on the wood floor impatiently as she opened the door to the closet.

"What do you think I am, an imbecile?" he yelled when she began to sift through the items inside it.

Even though she should have been prepared for this kind of reaction, Sara still flinched. "No, Geoff." She kept her voice low as she explained, "I guess I had to see for myself that it wasn't here. I'm sorry if my need to double-check made you feel I doubted you."

Her husband's sensual mouth twisted in disgust. "You're sorry, alright. What I ever saw in you, I'll never know. Now, what did you do with my jacket?"

"Geoff, I didn't do anything with it, I swear. The last time I saw it was when I hung it in here after I washed it on Monday. I checked the master closet, and it's not there, either."

"Fine," Geoff said, his tone implying that it wasn't "fine" at all. "I'll go without it, and then you can nurse the cold I'll most likely develop because I wasn't wearing it, you miserable excuse for a homemaker and even worse excuse for a wife!"

He stormed out of the house into the crisp, but not truly cold, early fall weather and Sara slowly let out the exasperated breath she hadn't realized she'd been holding. Geoff would probably find the missing jacket in his car or at the office, she was almost sure. Sighing, she returned to the task of ungunking Abby's hair.

As she climbed the stairs, memories of the night before assaulted her, of Geoff coming in late, his heavy hand on her shoulder jerking her out of a sound sleep, his breath smelling of scotch and his collar of another woman's perfume. Her startled reaction, to swing out in self-defense, was instinctive, not meant for anyone in particular, certainly not meant at all the way he took it—that she had no desire for him. He had rubbed his jaw where her flailing fist connected, called her "frigid", and shoved her roughly away from him — and she had been unable to convince him she felt otherwise, perhaps because it was true that she cringed from him in his inebriated state and because he smelled of scent she didn't wear — she couldn't help it.

Pulling herself back to the present moment, she finished up with her daughter. There was no "thank you" for her efforts when the peanut butter finally worked its magic. Abby only said rather rudely, "Alright, Mom, you can leave now. I need to get in the shower to wash my hair before I'm late for school."

When Sara exited the room, her twelve-year-old son, Aidan, in his mad dash to play *World of Warcraft* before he had to catch the bus, plowed right into her, and as he did so, his book bag — anchored on only one shoulder instead of both — swung out wildly and clipped her on the shoulder. Sara yelped and tears sprang to her eyes at the unexpected, jarring pain, but Aidan didn't look back, didn't even break his galloping stride. His mother was left standing alone, rubbing the spot where a large bruise was already beginning to swell and darken. Aidan, her baby, the child she'd coddled and cooed over, had turned into a miniature of his father, cold and distant, seemingly overnight, and Sara still couldn't fathom why. All she knew was that both children, as they had gotten older, had turned their backs on her, except when it suited them—then they demanded her attention in ways that made her feel like a servant. Well, what did she expect? Look who they were patterning themselves off of.

Fuming inwardly, Sara took herself off to the backyard as soon as the kids were gone. It seemed the only place she could find any solace these days. The soil didn't protest when she vented the anger she was afraid to show elsewhere by gouging at it forcefully with a hoe, and the flowers she intended to plant in the bed she was digging, when they bloomed deep pink against the snow of winter, would give her the comfort she couldn't get from her family.

As she hacked at the ground with the implement like a serial killer with an axe, the rain-softened dirt clods flew in all directions, and her next-door neighbor, Maritta, hands held protectively over her head, called over the fence, "Whoa there, Sara! What're you trying to do? Knock me out?"

Sara kept pounding the dirt mercilessly as she answered, her calm voice at odds with her frenetic actions, "No, just readying the ground for the camellias I want to plant."

"Looks to me like it's not only camellias you want to plant," Maritta said drily, propping her arms atop the fence. She quirked an eyebrow at the sight of the rectangular hole that looked more like a shallow grave than a flower bed.

Sara stopped, hoe mid-air, and stared down at the results of her furious efforts. A bubble of hysterical laughter nearly escaped her as she thought, for one split-second, that she'd like to "plant" a certain person in it, alright. Then guilt rose up in her throat and she choked on the disloyal thoughts. Geoff was right—she was a sorry excuse for a wife.

Deciding that very second to elongate the bed because she hadn't worked out all her frustrations yet, Sara moved a foot or so over to unbroken ground and struck it with all her might while Maritta watched. That same instant, something flew up and hit her smack in the eye. "Yeowch!" she yelped, throwing down the hoe to cup the injury with her right hand.

"Oh my gosh, you're bleeding!" Maritta exclaimed as a crimson stream escaped Sara's protective fingers and trickled down her cheek. "Don't move, Sara! I'll be right over!"

Maritta disappeared for a few seconds and reappeared, via the side gate, in Sara's yard holding a damp white cloth in her hand. "Here, wipe the drips off and then hold this tightly against the cut. It will stop the bleeding." She held the cloth out to Sara.

As Sara mopped her face and hand then folded the cloth so that a clean area was exposed. She held it to her eyelid gingerly. Maritta walked slowly around the area nearby, eyes focused on the ground.

"What are you doing?" Sara asked.

Maritta looked up and said, "I'm searching for whatever it was that hit you. That's a pretty nasty little cut you've got, and I wouldn't want anyone to step on the thing that caused it."

"Good thinking," Sara replied, feeling in the wrong (as always) that she hadn't been the one to consider protecting her family.

"This is weird," Maritta muttered as she bent down and picked something up.

"What's weird?"

"Well, the only thing I've found so far is this dirty old coin." Maritta held up the object in question. "But it's round, so how could it have cut you like that?"

"It flew up hard and fast, that's how. It didn't slice so much as the force of the impact tore my skin apart. May I see it?" Sara held out her unoccupied hand.

"Sure," Maritta said, dropping the coin into Sara's palm.

"It doesn't look like it's from this country." Sara examined the ancient lyre on one side. She flipped it over to see the numbers 1 and 2 stamped vertically, the 2 below the 1, in the center of the coin, with strange script beneath them. As she rotated the coin in her fingers the word "Israel" stood out clearly along the outer edge sandwiched in between more of the unrecognizable lettering. "It's from Israel!" she exclaimed.

"Let me see." Maritta took the coin back. She frowned in concentration as she studied the object more closely. "Hmm, what does this remind me of? Oh, I know! The parable in the Bible about the five talents."

"What do talents have to do with a coin from Israel?" Sara asked.

"In Jesus's parable the talents are coins," Maritta replied.

"Oh…I get it now," Sara said, but she really didn't, so after Maritta left, she went inside and put the coin on the counter next to the sink where she would wash it later. From there, she entered the half-bath off the kitchen, cleaned the wound just below her left eyebrow with antiseptic, saw in the mirror that it wasn't as bad as Maritta made it out to be (facial cuts tended to bleed more profusely), and used a butterfly bandage to close it, then went to the bookcase in the living room and got out the old Bible that used to be her grandfather's.

Just touching the crumbling black cover brought back memories of her childhood and attending church on Sundays with her grandparents. Sara hadn't gone to church in twenty years now, because Geoff was agnostic. He rarely went to church with her when they had been dating, and, once they were married, he flatly refused to accompany her at all anymore. He also insisted that they not force religion on their children once they were born, so, after awhile, she stopped going, too.

Sara pulled her attention back to the present and the tome she held in her hands. Turning to the New Testament, she gently leafed through the thin, tissue-like pages—first the Index, and then the gospel of St. Matthew, scanning the red print until she located the parable.

As she read the story, the verse in which the master gave his servants "talents" according to their abilities jumped out at her. It still seemed to her as though the "talents" were "gifts", not "money", and her heart gave a strange lurch. She continued on and felt an actual constriction in her chest when she reached the part where the man with only one talent hid it in the earth. The tightness spread upward into her throat—ironic, since her one, long-unused talent was to sing like a nightingale. By the time Sara reached the end of the parable, when the master took everything away from the man who hid that talent, she felt all choked up, as though she couldn't breathe, and she would have thrown the book across the room had it not been a fragile, treasured possession.

She had the epiphany in that moment that she had hidden her talent in the earth, too, substituting gardening for singing, since it was an occupation deemed worthy of her efforts by her husband.

Easing the Bible carefully back into its slot in the bookcase, Sara returned to the kitchen sink where she washed the coin off in a daze. When it was clean and dry, she took it to the kitchen table and sank down onto one of the padded wooden chairs where she just sat and stared at it.

What were the odds of a Jewish coin turning up in her Midwestern backyard? She thought it stranger still that she should be struck by that "talent" with such force and that her neighbor would be reminded of the parable just by seeing the coin. It certainly seemed that Someone Up There was trying to tell her something, and it didn't take an ant's brains to decipher what that something was. Sara wasn't using her talent; therefore, she was going to lose it.

People had always told her that her voice was heaven-sent, that of a living angel. When she was a little girl, she had no doubt that they were right, and she delighted in singing in the choir. As she got older, those who heard her warble always insisted that she should cut an album because, they said, she was even better than Amy Grant. And in her heart of hearts, Sara had wanted to do just that. Then she met Geoff, charming Geoff, who at first championed her and said he was going to do all he could to help her reach stardom then little by little crushed her dreams beneath his disapproving heel. He'd tell her she was off-key, or that he was tired and just wanted some peace when he came in from work to find her singing. Before long, he didn't want to hear her sing at all. And she had taken his dismissal even deeper and buried her hopes far, far underground…

Sara tried to remember when she'd last sung. It had to have been before Aidan was born. She hadn't even listened to the radio much since then because it made her want to sing along, and that was a "no-no". As she thought about how sterile and depressing her life had become over the past twelve years, a small but strong voice from within said, "Why is using what God gave you a 'no-no'? What about the parable? Which is worse? Not honoring your husband? Or not honoring the Master?"

"Not honoring You," Sara whispered. As soon as the words left her lips, it felt as though a dam within her had broken. She got up from the table and went into the computer room to look up her old church on the Internet. Sunday services used to start at 9:00 a.m. but she couldn't even be sure that the church was still in existence after all these years, let alone that the times for the worship services were still the same.

Sara typed in the name in the search engine. It came right up, and she saw that the sermon times were the same as they used to be. She jotted down the number and the address, even though they hadn't changed, and slipped the piece of paper into her wallet. Then she hummed under her breath. The sounds were tentative—the old "pipes" were definitely rusty—but she was going to use them, anyway, and she refused to think about how Geoff would react, both to her singing again and to her return to church and the choir.

Chapter 2

When Sunday morning came, Sara was up early, before anyone else in the house was awake. She had showered the night before, and now she tiptoed to the walk-in closet and took out the dress and shoes she'd put to the forefront of her area of the closet the night before, then crept downstairs to the half-bath where she had tucked makeup, jewelry, and other grooming aids away behind the extra toilet tissue and completed her preparations for church. She wrote a note saying that she would be back around 11:00 a.m. and would fix brunch for everyone then and left it on the kitchen table. Sending up a silent prayer that none of them would rouse until around 10:30 (as was usual), she let herself out of the house with a slight snick of the door that led to the garage.

Sara held her breath when she pushed the button next to the light switch that opened the garage door. If it made too much noise, she wouldn't get away without waking someone, and she just didn't want to deal with their complaints that she wasn't going to be as available to them today. She especially didn't want to have to deal with Geoff — not until this little foray was a fait accompli, anyway. She blew the breath out forcefully enough to lift her bangs when the opener, sometimes cranky, worked smoothly — and almost silently — this time.

Jumping into her sedate, tan Toyota Camry (she'd wanted a bright metallic blue one but Geoff, who controlled the finances, nixed that on the basis that the color would attract the attention of the highway patrol more easily), Sara backed out, leaving the garage door wide open. She'd turned the lock on the door leading into the house before she closed it, so that would just have to do. She wasn't about to take the chance that the garage door would close as silently as it opened, even though she dreaded the fit Geoff was going to pitch about her carelessness when she got back.

But truly, in their neighborhood, such caution was unnecessary. They all looked out for one another, and thefts were virtually non-existent. She could just hear Geoff yelling, "Well there's always a first time, Sara!" and "My car could have been stolen!" and "My golf clubs and the kids' bikes were left sitting in plain view where anyone could take them!"

None of that mattered now. What was important was that Sara was taking a new lease out on life. She couldn't wait to return to the fold, to her old friends (if any were still in attendance) and to the choir. As soon as she arrived at church today, she intended to find the choir director and offer her talent to them again. As she drove, she looked out the car windows at the beautiful autumn leaves on the trees in varying shades of purple, brown, red, orange, yellow, and green, at the cerulean blue sky dotted with a few wispy clouds, at the sun shining so brilliantly, and she burst into song, just like the warbler she'd seen sitting on the branch of one of the maples she passed.

It felt so good use her gift that she almost cried. Within minutes she reached her destination, but it felt as though she'd flown there in seconds.

As Sara pulled into the parking lot next to the old white church with its white spire and arched stained-glass windows, the wonderful feeling in her heart persisted, and it spread all throughout her body when she recognized her old pastor, Pastor Dan, standing at the door, greeting all the early bird arrivals. Then she saw her same choir director, Jana Campobello, in the choir loft above the pulpit as she entered the building. She all but flew up the stairs to the loft.

"Why, if it isn't Sara Avery!" Jana, a fifty-something woman who still had bold red hair, exclaimed in surprise, throwing her arms open wide with a big smile. "Where have you been all these years, woman?" she asked as she gave Sara a warm, welcoming hug.

"I've been busy with my home and family." The feeble excuse made Sara feel ashamed as she hugged Jana back.

She expected her former mentor to jump all over that

pitiful pretext and ask her why she didn't bring her family with her to church — both back then and today — but the choir director only held her more tightly and said, "I so loved your voice, and I never thought I'd ever hear it again, figured you'd moved away. I sure have missed you. And I hope you're not too 'busy' to rejoin us now."

Sara pulled back so she could see Jana's face when she told her, "Actually, that's exactly why I came today. I've missed you and the choir more than you'll ever know, and I was praying you'd have room for me to rejoin you."

Jana's smile could have lit up the entire loft as she replied, "There's always room for you, sweetie. And we'd make room if there wasn't. Are you able to do the pre-service practice and jump in with us this morning?"

"You betcha!"

This morning the choir was only singing two songs, since there was also a special guest singer to complement the new series of sermons Pastor Dan was giving on finding yourself in the Lord. One of the songs, "In the Garden" was a traditional favorite of Sara's and the other, "Awesome God," was one that was new in 1988, when she was a kid, long before she ever met Geoff or quit the choir, so she knew that one, too, and had no problem catching up in the limited practice time.

When the first sermon was over, Sara hung the purple satin robe back up in the closet and gathered her purse and sweater in preparation to leave.

Jana, whose attention had been centered on a choir member who was having difficulty hitting some of the notes, turned and caught her in the act of sneaking out. "Where are you going, Sara? Aren't you staying for second session?"

Sara blushed and stammered, "I...I really can't this morning, Jana. I hadn't planned on singing first service, as it was. I only meant to speak with you about reconnecting and maybe stay for part of the service, not the entire thing. I have to get back now, but I'll call you — now that I have your number again — later this afternoon and get practice times from you. I'll be better prepared next Sunday, promise!"

"You were awesome this Sunday, Sara, even without much practice. I'm just sorry the second bunch will miss out on the treat that the first bunch got."

"I'm sorry, too, but I left my family sleeping and they'll be wanting their breakfast."

"Let them make their own breakfast next Sunday, or better yet, bring them with you!" Jana invited.

"We'll see..." Sara said vaguely and scooted down the loft stairs before Jana could wrangle a more definite promise out of her. The day any of her family set foot in church would be a miraculous day, indeed.

Her drive home was not the joyous ride the trip there had been. As soon as she got back into her Camry all the good feeling that being in choir and Pastor Dan's sermon had filled her with suddenly evaporated, as if she'd swallowed a spoonful of calcium chloride. The closer she came to her own driveway, the more she felt like turning the car around and just taking off to any place that wasn't home. But, Sara knew that she had to return (she refused to think of it as "facing the music") sooner or later, and that the later she did so, the worse what awaited her would be, so best to get it over with now. Still, her heart plummeted to the toe of her left shoe as she stepped out of the car.

The garage was closed when she pulled up and she had to reopen it, so she knew Geoff had caught on to the fact that she'd left it open already. Mentally bracing herself, she turned the knob on the inner door to the house, giving it a slight shove. Geoff and the kids sat at the kitchen table wearing their pajamas and matching disgruntled expressions.

"Where the heck have you been, Sara?" Geoff demanded to know.

"Out," Sara answered succinctly. She took her sweater off and hung it over the back of the remaining empty chair, then asked, "Did you all just finish eating, then?"

"What? Are you crazy?" Geoff barked. "We've been waiting for you to show up to make our Sunday breakfast. I thought you'd gone to the store for something, but, obviously, you didn't do that. And you left the garage door open. Doggone it, Sara! If I've told you once, I've told you a thousand times—that kind of carelessness is going to cost us big time someday. Lots of sticky fingers out there, just waiting to snatch our unprotected stuff."

"Yeah, Mom," both kids said, though whether they were agreeing with Geoff about the garage door or about having to wait for their breakfast was unclear.

"Sorry," Sara said simply, as she rolled up her sleeves and began taking removing items from the refrigerator and cupboards.

Geoff's face darkened as the thunderhead began to form. "That's all you have to say—'sorry'? I want to know where you disappeared to if not to the market."

"That's private," Sara said, measuring pancake mix into a bowl.

The storm unleashed. "Private! You're my wife; there's nothing 'private' in marriage!" Geoff yelled.

"Isn't there?" Sara asked quietly, shooting him a look as the memory of his perfumed collar rose up to stand between them. From the look on Geoff's face, he got her meaning because he backed off somewhat, although not completely.

"Look, we just want to know what was so important that you weren't here to share family morning with us," he said on a sigh.

"If you really must know, I went to church," Sara answered. "I rejoined choir. And I will be gone every Sunday morning from now until forever," she insisted, chin held high. She broke an egg into the pan and started to hum to the tune of, "Our God is an Awesome God."

Abby's mouth dropped open in astonishment, and Aidan said, "You sing, Mom?"

"I used to, before you were born, and I do now, too." She hitched her chin a little higher and sang a line of the song outright.

"Well don't expect us to get up and go with you to some funky old church filled with a bunch of old people," Abby declared, wrinkling her perfect little nose in disdain.

"Then don't expect me to come back and fix you all breakfast, either!" her mother retorted. For a second Sara looked as shocked as the rest of them did when the words welled up and out of her of their own accord. Then she straightened her spine and added, "You are all capable of learning to cook, so after this morning, on Sundays, you're on your own. I'll make us all family breakfast on Saturday, instead."

"I think I might like to come with you next Sunday, Mom," Aidan surprised her by saying. "I want to hear you sing. What I heard just now sounded pretty good."

"It will mean getting up early and sitting through two sermons, because I have choir duty during both," Sara told him, whisking the batter in the blue ceramic bowl she held.

"That's okay, I want to hear you sing," Aidan repeated, looking at her seriously. Sara wanted to go over and hug him right that instant, but Geoff's next remark froze her in place.

"Well, I don't want to hear you sing, and I don't want to hear you hum, either! If you insist on doing this, then you'll do it outside this house." He stood up abruptly, the legs of his chair scraping the tile floor in the same ear-splitting way fingernails rake a blackboard. "You all enjoy your breakfast— I've lost my appetite. I'm off to play golf. I'll be back when I get back." And he stalked out of the room, slamming the door that led to the garage behind him.

As soon as he left, Sara turned the radio on in the kitchen and finished making pancakes and sausage for her children. When a song came on that she knew, she sang along defiantly. Both children looked astonished. "Wow, Mom, you can really sing!" Abby breathed. "Wonder why Dad doesn't want you to?"

Because he's afraid I'll get rich and famous and leave him, Sara thought, but didn't give voice to the realization. She wouldn't leave, no matter how bad it got, because she took her marriage vows — for better or for worse — seriously, but she also knew, deep within, that her days of being a doormat were over for good. God wanted her to sing, and sing she would. Not only that, but she *would* record, if the opportunity ever arose again.

Chapter 3

The following Sunday, Sara didn't try to hide her movements. She rapped on Aidan's door to wake him, then freely readied herself for church and went downstairs to fix something quick and easy for her son and herself. Five minutes later, both children appeared in the kitchen, fully dressed.

Sara sent Abby an arch look and said, "I thought you didn't want to come with me to 'some funky old church filled with a bunch of old people'."

"That was before I heard you sing, Mom," Abby said, eyeing her mother with newfound respect.

Sara hid the smile that quirked at the corners of her lips by busying herself with pouring three glasses of orange juice to go with the toaster strudel and microwaveable sausages she'd rustled up. "Here, Abby, put these on the table for us while I make a couple more strudels for you, okay?"

Amazingly, her daughter did as she was bidden without one huff of complaint.

After breakfast, Sara went to the bookcase and got out Grandpa's Bible. She'd left it behind in the rush to escape undiscovered last Sunday, but now she wanted to bring it along. It just felt right that she should do so. As she pulled it off the shelf, a piece of paper dislodged itself from the pages and fluttered to the floor.

Picking it up, Sara read: "Sing unto the Lord a new song and His praise from the end of the earth... Isaiah 42:10" The words, God's words, were written in her grandpa's spidery hand, and, to Sara, it felt like a benediction from both God and her beloved ancestor. If ever there was a sign that she was meant to do what she was finally doing, this was it. Tears of joy leaked from her eyes, and she drove herself and the children to church in a happy daze.

At the church, she introduced Abby and Aidan to her friends then showed them where the teens sat in a special section in the pews. "Wednesday evenings used to be Teen Night. If it still is, and you're interested in checking it out, I can bring you," she told them.

"But Aidan isn't a teen yet, Mom," Abby protested, flipping her long blonde hair back and batting her eyelashes at a cute boy with wavy brown hair and melted chocolate brown eyes who sat at the opposite end of the row she stood next to.

"Well, Teen Night was sort of a misnomer, because it actually included middle-school kids, too. The church wasn't big enough to have separate programs for each group."

"Cool," Abby said, sending a dazzling smile the boy's way. "I think I might want to go, if they still have it. How about you, Aidan?"

"Yeah, that might be fun," Aidan agreed, waving at another boy about his age whom he apparently already knew.

"Well, you two settle in, and we'll talk about it on the way home. I've got to get up to the loft now."

During the two worship services, Sara's voice soared over the others' in the choir. She didn't mean to upstage them; it just happened. She sang as she had never before sung in her entire life — "a new song unto the Lord." As her words rang in the rafters above her, she looked out over the congregation. Every member looked up toward her with rapt faces, including her children. Her heart swelled with the notes of her song, and she had never felt so fulfilled.

They liked to never have got away after the second sermon ended. Everyone wanted to come up to her and shake her hand, or give her a hug, or pat her on the back in encouragement. Everyone said how blown away they were by her talent, including the other choir members. Sara thought the absolute topper of the morning was when the director of the music program, Ron Jamison, said he was going to talk to a friend of his who owned a recording studio — "A voice like yours is a gift to the world; you can't just hide it away in this little church, much as we love hearing it. You must record!" — but she was wrong. The absolute zenith of the day was reached as Sara drove them home again.

"Mom, you were awesome!" both kids exclaimed in unison, the moment the car doors slammed behind them, sealing them all inside away from the world.

She glanced over at Abby in the front seat. Her daughter was smiling at her in a way she hadn't done since she was in third grade, with love, admiration, and yes, respect, in her eyes. She looked in the rearview mirror at Aidan, and he wore an identical expression.

"Don't let Dad stop you from singing ever again, Mom," Abby said in a tone that said she'd stand behind her mother, another first in a long time.

"I agree. Dad should be proud of you, not try to shut you up. And I agree with Mr. Jamison. You *should* record. You'll be famous," Aidan declared, crossing his arms over his chest in a gesture of finality, as if Sara's fate was a done deal.

Sara wasn't so sure she'd ever do anything more than what she was doing now with her voice. After all, she didn't want to put her marriage in jeopardy. She was just happy that she was singing again. That was enough for her.

It was a good thing that Sara had extra joy in her heart— otherwise every bit of it would have been leached out by Geoff's distant attitude when they got home. The kids were all fired up over what happened and jabbered on about how great their mother was and how much fun it had been to go to church, how they had seen some old friends there and made some new ones, and how they definitely wanted to go to Teen Night this upcoming Wednesday.

As they talked excitedly, neither one of them noticed that their father hadn't uttered a word, but they did notice when he barked, "No way! You're not going. You were lucky I allowed this one-time trip to church, but I'll be hanged if any child of mine is going to get sucked into some subservient cult!"

"It's not a cult, Dad; it's a church full of really nice people," Abby burst out then stopped and chewed nervously on her lower lip.

"I *said*, you're not going." Geoff's tone was deadly quiet.

"How is forbidding them to go to church any different than attending a 'subservient cult'?" Sara confronted him, hands on hips. "Aren't they being forced to bend to *your* will, as opposed to God's will? I say they can go if they want to."

Geoff glared fiercely at Sara and then stomped upstairs to the movie den where he hid out for the remainder of the day and watched football on the big screen TV there. Sara tried to appease him by bringing him an iced drink and some peanuts, but he didn't even look her way when she sat them down on the coffee table in front of him. And, when they went to bed that night he turned a cold back to her and violently shrugged the tentative hand she placed on his shoulder off. She sighed and turned on her side away from him. No matter how he acted, she wasn't giving in. Not this time, not about singing, and not about allowing the children to choose for themselves how they would worship. After all, that right was the very foundation of the nation.

Chapter 4

Sara attended choir practice during the day on Monday, and when Wednesday evening rolled around, she fixed an easy, early supper for her and the children—taco salad—before writing a note for Geoff. (They left for church at 5:30 and Geoff never got home before 6:00.) The choir had an evening practice on Wednesdays, as several of the choir members worked, and those who were parents brought their pre-teens and teens to Teen Night while they squeezed in the only other practice—besides early Sunday mornings before service—that they could.

They were to practice a song by the number one Christian rock recording star, Mandisa, and Sara was nervous about it. Since she'd cut herself off from all music rather than feel the sting of not being able to sing, she had no idea who Mandisa was, or what kind of songs he or she did. But when Jana played the song from the CD, Sara instantly knew this was her song, and when it came time for the choir to sing a round-robin rendition of it that Jana had printed out for them, Sara sang her heart out.

It gratified her greatly that all the kids on the premises that night came in to hear the choir sing. "Wow," Kimberly

Eagan whispered in an aside to Sara as all voices stilled at their appearance, "this just never happens, the kids wanting to stop whatever they've got going to come and check us out. Guess it's because you're here."

Shaking her head in disbelief, Sara replied, "Oh, I don't think so."

She was about to add that she was sure they had each come to hear their own family members when one of the older boys, the one she was pretty sure Abby had a crush on, pointed straight at her and said, "There she is! She has got the best set of tailpipes I've ever heard on a woman. Listen up, you guys!"

Though Sara concealed a smile at the way the kid called them her "tailpipes" instead of "pipes", she felt a warm glow spread throughout her entire being. Abby stepped out from behind the boy and called, "Rock out, Mom! We came to hear you sing 'Stronger' by Mandisa again."

"Is that okay with everybody?" Sara quirked a questioning brow at Jana first, and then looked around to include the rest of the choir in her request.

"Is that okay with us?" Jana laughed. "Of course, it's okay with us! The kids have graced us all with their presence, so now you must grace them, too." She held a pitch pipe up to her lips and blew into it. Sara began, and the rest of the group chimed in at different times under Jana's direction. The second rendition nearly took the roof off the building, and that was without any backup instruments.

The kids stomped and cheered and whistled. Several of them even took out their cell phones and held them up, lights on, just as if they were at a concert. Then they all started yelling, "More! We want more!"

At Jana's direction both voices and instruments were lifted. Once again, Sara's voice rang out over the others as she sang about the waves that threatened to take us under, and, in the middle of that third take, Ron Jamison walked in. When the song was finished, he strolled up to the platform where the choir stood with an amazed expression on his face.

"I insist that the choir, especially you Sara, practice this particular song to record. I'll arrange the sound room, and I think that the choir should also do some other contemporary Christian songs as well as a couple of the newer Christian Christmas songs—like Kari Jobe's 'Adore Him'—and cut a complete album of ten to twelve songs when you visit the studio. We'll sell more if we have Christmas songs on it at this time of year. I'm jazzed because, for the first time in years, this choir sounds like it's on fire. Maybe Sara's given you all something to compete with or to aspire to. Whatever it is, the choir sounded awesome just now." Then he turned to the band and added, "And you, all of you, were completely in tune and in time with the singers, even though the arrangement was round robin. Great job! Of course, you'll back the choir up, so keep up the good work.

"I'll let you know when I can get an all day Saturday slot. It will probably take a month to a month and a half to nail it down. I know that doesn't give you a lot of time, so you'll have to readjust your schedules and practice every day to get the material ready. Then we'll go into the production of the CD's and marketing so that, hopefully, we'll eventually have a gold or platinum bestseller, and a great Christmas gift for this year. Just don't let me down by being anything less than what I just heard — your absolute best," Jamison told them all with a smile and a thumbs up before he took a seat in the pews to listen to the rest of the practice.

Afterward, everyone stayed for coffee and cookies. The room was abuzz with a mixture of both excitement and trepidation over the upcoming project. "A recording! Imagine, we're gonna be recorded!" "Hey, that reminds me of another great song we can do — 'I Can Only Imagine'." "Yeah, and how about 'Blessed be the Name'? That's another really good one." "I don't know how I can squeeze in all these extra practices — I'm overloaded as it is." "Oh, you'll survive. It's only for something like six weeks — you heard Ron. You can do six weeks." "I've got other commitments. Guess I'll have to put them off, though. The Lord comes first. And this opportunity is heaven sent."

As Sara listened to the others, she felt the waves she'd just sung about threatening to rise up and overwhelm her. How was she ever going to keep up? She didn't know any of these songs. But then Aidan, who was standing next to her wolfing down an Oreo and sipping the punch put out for the kids, looked up, took in her brows pleated together with anxiety and her teeth as they worried her bottom lip and said, "Don't sweat it, Mom. We can look the songs up for you on the Internet and download them so you have them to practice with at home. You're so good, you'll catch up with the others in no time."

"Thanks, sweetie," Sara said, but her boy didn't know that her ignorance of modern music was only a miniscule part of what was upsetting her. What bothered her most was the thought of Geoff's reaction to the practices she would now have to attend every day now, and also to the recording that would come at the end of it all.

Her fears were justified.

* * *

Geoff came unhinged when she told him. She'd seen him angry before, but she'd never seen him like this. "NO!" he exploded, slamming his fist so hard into the wall nearby that it put a hole in it. His eyes flashed like warning lights as his fury spewed forth. "I say NO! This whole church thing has gotten out of hand and it's gone far enough! You are my wife and you have a duty to me and the family first! You do this thing against my will, Sara, and I promise you, you'll live to regret it! No more church, not for you or for the kids, and I want dinner on the table when I get home from now on!"

Sara bit her tongue to keep from arguing, *And when might that be? You're never here by the time dinner is on the table most nights.*

He snatched up his car keys from the island in the kitchen, and as always when things didn't go as he expected, stormed out, leaving Sara and the kids standing stalk still in the wake of his explosion.

After several shocked seconds, they began to regain their equanimity. Abby spoke first. "You can't let him stop you, Mom! This is your chance to shine."

"But your father has a point, Abby. He is my husband, and I do have a duty to him and to you two. How do I tend to that and still keep up with all the practices?" Sara shook her head sadly. "There's no way. I'll just have to drop out."

Aidan, the youngest of them all, was the voice of wisdom. "But if you drop out, then the recording won't happen, and the other choir members will lose their chance to send their talents out into the world, too. You can't do that to them. It's not fair. There has to be a way!" He declared earnestly.

"Aidan's right, Mom. There has to be a way, so don't do anything drastic like calling Jana and quitting just yet. Let's all put on our thinking caps and do some brainstorming, like we've done in the past when there's been a problem we couldn't solve on our own."

Sara knew that her children were right. She couldn't let the choir down, but she couldn't let her husband down and hope to keep her marriage intact, either. "Okay," she relented. "Let's make some hot cocoa and go sit by the fire in the den. I'll let you two stay up just another hour. Maybe we can come up with a solution in that time."

"If we don't, I say we sleep on it, and wrack our brains all day tomorrow, too. Don't talk to Jana until we get home from school, Mom, please. Give it as much time as we can, first," Abby pleaded.

"Are you sure you're not doing this because of a certain boy with Hershey's kisses eyes?" Sara teased her lightly.

"No, Mom!" Abby protested, blushing.

Chuckling, Sara hugged her daughter and said, "Just kidding, sweetie. I know you and Aidan have only the purest of motives for helping me, so why don't you start now by helping me make the cocoa?"

There wasn't much to the preparation. Sara kept boxes of Nestlé's hot chocolate with marshmallows in microwavable packets on hand. Abby got down three mugs and filled them with milk, and after Sara handed him the box, Aidan tore open three packets and carefully poured them into each mug. Sara stirred each one with a small wire whisk and put all three cups into the large, built-in microwave next to the kitchen cabinets. In less than two minutes, they were trooping into the den, Sara carrying the three mugs on a tray.

When they were all situated comfortably on the big overstuffed couch with fleece lap blankets tucked around them and mugs in hand, Sara said, "Okay, time to brainstorm. Just relax, put on those thinking caps, and say whatever comes to mind."

"What if Aidan and I learn to cook some easy stuff and we feed Daddy his dinner while you practice?" Abby asked after a minute or two went by. "Except Wednesdays, of course. I still want to go to Teen Night."

"Or what if we order out and have it ready for Dad when he gets home?" Aidan rode on the heels of Abby's thought. "And I want to go to Teen Night, too, so what could we do on Wednesdays?"

"Good suggestions, both of them," Sara said. "The

ordering out could work for Wednesdays. I think part of what made your Dad so mad tonight was that we ate dinner together and left him to fend for himself." She didn't say that it was probably the smallest piece of tinder that set fire to Geoff's ire. Nor did she reveal how uncomfortable she was with forging ahead with this plan. What good would it serve to make the children a party to her misgivings?

Abby showed unusual sensitivity when she questioned, "But won't Daddy still be mad that you're not there to eat with us? Even if we make him dinner? How do we fix that?"

"We don't. That's something he has to fix for himself. We're not responsible for his feelings." The assertion came from somewhere deep inside Sara's psyche, and the words were a long overdue pardon from the imprisoning feelings of misplaced responsibility and guilt that she'd trapped herself in for years. In her attempt to protect her children from wrongheaded thinking just now, she finally realized what she'd done — or allowed Geoff to do to her — over the past fifteen years. "So," she added briskly, "We just let your father deal with his feelings in his own way, and until and unless he sees a better way, we don't feel bad about it, okay?"

The kids' expressions were a mixture of relief and doubt, sort of like opposing theatre masks. Sara had no doubt the look on her own face was similar. But she finally saw her husband for the bullying tyrant he was, acting like a spoiled kid and throwing tantrums whenever things didn't go his way.

Chapter 5

Geoff came staggering in at 3:00 a.m. The racket he made as he stumbled around woke Sara up. Throwing off the blankets, grabbing her robe, and stuffing her feet into furry slippers, Sara hurried downstairs hoping against hope that he hadn't awoken the children, too. They had school and needed their sleep.

"Geoff, what are you doing? You're going to wake the kids," Sara said as she entered the kitchen.

Geoff had his head stuck in the refrigerator, but he yanked it back out when he heard her. Turning, he glared at his wife with bloodshot eyes. *Oh no, not again*, Sara thought, closing her eyes.

"I'm getting myself something to eat—are you blind?" he snarled, his voice still way too loud.

"Fine, but can you tone it down, please? Abby and Aidan have to get up in just a few hours."

"'Abby and Aidan have to get up in just a few hours'," he mocked childishly with an ugly sneer on his face. "Why should I care, hmmm? Nobody in this house cares how I feel anymore!"

When he was in this state, nothing penetrated; it was

useless to argue with him. And while she did care, too much, about what her husband felt, a small rebellious part of her whispered inwardly, *He's never cared what any of the rest of us felt, why **should** we care?* "That's not true, Geoff," ~~Abby~~ Sara said quietly, although she knew from experience that her words would go unheeded and he would continue to rant.

Geoff pulled cold cuts, cheese and condiments from the fridge and slammed them on the marble topped island so hard he almost broke the jar of mayonnaise. "No one cares," he reiterated loudly, "especially not you, you cold, frigid, selfish—!"

"Geoff, please!" she cut him off before he could utter what she knew would be a vulgar word.

"'Geoff please!'" he mimicked again. "Please what, Sara? Please shove my—"

Slapping her hands over her ears, Sara screamed, "STOP IT!" at the top of her powerful lungs. Then the kids did awaken and came rushing, all disheveled, into the room.

"Mom, what's wrong?" they cried, their faces etched with fear.

"Nothing," she replied tonelessly. Then, inhaling deeply, she straightened her shoulders. "Grab your coats and shoes; you're taking a day off school, and we're leaving this house."

"Go ahead, leave! All of you! See if I care!" Geoff stormed.

The kids quickly and silently did as their mother said and within minutes they were driving away. As if their father could still hear them while the house remained in view, they waited until Sara turned a corner to speak.

"We're not leaving for good, are we, Mom?" Aidan asked from the backseat.

"No, honey, but none of us should have to listen to your father when he's like this anymore. We never did deserve it, and it's my fault I didn't do this sooner. We're just going to a hotel where we can lounge around in our pajamas until your dad leaves for work, and then we'll go home again. I'll let you both play hooky and we'll have a fun day. We'll play some games and I'll teach you each how to cook. Aidan, you can make lunch, and Abby, you'll prepare dinner with my assistance. Then I'll have to leave for choir practice."

"But what if Dad is still this mad when he comes home from work?" Aidan's voice quavered.

"I can't back down, Aidan. You said it yourself. Both of you have my cell number. If your dad gets out of hand, you just call me. I'll come right back, and we'll do this again…and again…as many times as it takes until your father sees that we just won't be there at all until and unless he calms down and treats us decently." Sara was stunned that this solution had presented itself so easily. Where was all this coming from?

It was like she was a completely different person than the one she'd been before the coin literally opened her eyes.

* * *

Since their sleep had been disrupted, Sara decided that it would be okay if they slept in until 9:00 at the hotel and then stayed there until 11:00; that way chances were better that they wouldn't run into Geoff — even if he, too, decided to play hooky, he'd more than likely go golfing and so he'd be gone by the time they got home.

After arising at the ring of the alarm clock, they took turns showering and then ordered a room service breakfast since none of them were dressed for public appearance. It felt strange to settle the bill and leave the hotel still clad in their nightclothes, as though everyone were staring at them (and they probably were), but there wasn't anything they could do to change it. When they reached their driveway, they were thankful that they had a garage they could drive into and close the door before getting out of the car — at least none of the neighbors would see them this way and start gossiping.

They spent the day as planned the night before since the man of the house was indeed, gone. When they tired of playing games, Aidan made sandwiches and they watched TV until three. Then Sara said, "Time for your first cooking lesson, Abby." She got up and held out a hand to her daughter who was still sprawled out on the sofa in the upstairs TV nook. Once Abby would have scowled and refused her help, but today, she merely put her hand in her mother's and asked, "What are we making?"

"Well, everybody likes my easy lasagna, and it reheats well, so that's what we'll do." She called down the hall to Aidan, who was off playing video games in his room, "Aidan! You can help, too. I'll teach you how to make the salad and garlic bread."

Normally, Aidan would have pitched a fit at having to stop in the middle of his game, but there was no argument from him. He quickly and willingly joined them. It seemed both kids had also undergone some sort of transformation and were nothing like they'd been before the coin incident, either. It seemed miracles did happen.

They were laughing and talking and working together to get dinner on the table by 4:30 so that Sara wouldn't have to gulp it down. Practice started at 6:00 each evening and went until 9:00 since there was such a limited time to become well-rehearsed. Aidan had just carried the salad bowl into the dining room and was returning to the kitchen, Abby was placing the toasted garlic bread on a plate, and Sara was slicing the lasagna for easier removal from the pan when the sound of the garage door opening reached their ears.

Everyone froze in their tracks and looked at each other in a panic. Geoff was home early, something that never happened these days.

"Oh great," Abby muttered under her breath.

"Uh-oh," Aidan whispered.

Sara pulled herself together and said with a confidence she didn't feel, "It'll be alright kids, I promise. You know how your father is. He growls and carries on, but it's all over the next day."

"Yeah, but that was before we went on strike," Abby said.

Geoff opened the door leading from garage to kitchen. There was instant silence and the kids slid wary glances at him.

"What?" he said, staring at each of them in turn. "Can't a man come home early once in awhile?"

Sara was an old hand at smoothing the waters, so she smiled brightly and said, "Well, you're just in time for dinner. Lasagna, salad and garlic bread."

"Good, I'm hungry. Felt like taking a day off work and going golfing. Been out all day. Even got a couple of holes in one." Geoff's smile was genuine, and Sara felt a pang as she realized how long it had been since she'd seen him like that. It made her miss him the way he used to be a long time ago.

"I made the lasagna, Daddy," Abby offered. "I hope you

like it."

As they all sat down together at the table for dinner the first time in months, Geoff speared Sara with suspicious eyes but only said, "If you made it honey, I'm sure it will be wonderful."

"And I made the salad and garlic bread, Dad," Aidan said, grabbing for the first piece of said bread.

"And what did Mommy do, huh?" Geoff's amiable mood slipped away. The spatula full of lasagna that he held hit his plate with a loud clink.

"Mom taught us how to cook, that's what she did," Abby defended.

"And why did Mommy think you two needed to learn to do her work?" he asked in an ominous tone.

"Please, Geoff, can't we for once in a blue moon, have a nice meal together? Is it such a crime that the kids wanted to learn to cook something and that I showed them how to make a couple of things? They're going to have to learn someday."

"Yeah, but why all of a sudden today?" Geoff challenged, his brows lowering.

There was no hope of salvaging the meal now. Sara swallowed the bite of lasagna she'd just taken with difficulty and sat up straight in her chair to say, "Because I'm going to choir practice tonight, and tomorrow night and all the nights to come for the next month and a half, that's why. The children wanted to help make it easier for us both. And they're coming with me on Wednesdays and Sundays."

"Oh, no they're not!" Geoff thundered. "Over my dead body!" He stood abruptly, knocking his chair to the floor. He deliberately flipped his plate over so that the lasagna with its red tomato sauce puddled, staining the white lace tablecloth.

"But Dad, we *want* to go!" both kids protested in unison.

"NO!" Geoff roared. "I said 'no' and that's final!"

Sara stood up, too, and said, "Abby, Aidan, get your coats. You're coming with me to practice."

The kids jumped at the chance to escape the room.

"I don't know what you think you're pulling here, Sara, but you're walking on thin ice that's getting thinner every minute! Keep it up, just keep it up and watch what happens!"

"Whatever happens can't be any worse than all the things I've put up with over the past fifteen years, Geoff," Sara retorted and walked away.

They stopped at a fast food place and ate burgers on the way since no one had gotten to finish their meal, and after choir practice, they returned home with every intention of spending another night in a hotel room if need be. None of them wanted to deal with Geoff as he'd been at supper.

However, when they got back it was to find that Geoff

had left again. Sara's heart sank as she surveyed the mess left on the dining room table. He hadn't even bothered to clean up before he took off, and now the salad was wilted, the lasagna that she'd hoped could feed them for at least two nights was dried up, as was the garlic bread. And the stain on the tablecloth, a wedding present from her grandma, would never come out now. She sent the kids on to bed with hugs and kisses—something they hadn't exchanged in years—and returned to the dining room alone.

Her mouth twisted grimly as she went to work, tossing out food, scraping and soaking the stuck on food from the dishes, and applying lemon juice to the stain in the tablecloth even though she knew this fix should have been applied much sooner. As she worked, her heart sped up with trepidation at the thought that there could be a replay of the previous night's events if Geoff had gone out drinking, something that was becoming a more frequent habit lately.

"Oh, God," she said aloud, "Thank you for giving me the fortitude to carry on and to overcome the problems that exist in my marriage. I don't know how this will be done, but I trust that You will help me find the way."

Sara was shocked anew at what left her mouth. She'd been intending to plead with her Higher Power to help her, to beg and bargain that if He took away Geoff's propensity to drink and womanize and to display such a nasty temper , she would do her best to get him to come to church. It would have been a prayer of the faithless, but instead, she had prayed a prayer that she recognized instantly as faith-filled, one of gratitude and trust. And, as she felt strength welling up within her, she knew exactly where it came from.

When Geoff came home in the state she'd more than half expected, she didn't get upset like she normally would have. Instead, a strange thing happened. She found herself filled with compassion for him, and though she inwardly recoiled at his sour whiskey breath, when he reached for her that night, she didn't flinch away, but opened her arms to him instead, loving the man that she knew to be in there somewhere despite his weaknesses.

Geoff, unfortunately, took that as a sign of her surrender — which it was not — so he was dumbfounded when he came home the following evening to a meal of hamburgers and potato chips prepared by his children, who were the only ones in evidence. Sara had already left for practice. He muttered under his breath, "If she thinks being all lovey-dovey to me is going to change how I feel about this, she's got another think coming."

He was waiting for her as she started to enter the house just after nine-thirty. "Hold on, let's have a little talk out here," he said, shutting the door to the garage behind him as he stepped out, barring her way in.

Sara felt a nervous flutter in her stomach, but she did her best not to go on the defensive. She sensed that trying to argue her case would be her downfall and that, if she ever hoped to reach her husband, she needed to stay calm and do her best to sympathize with his side of things without giving in. At least he was sober and able to see things more rationally now. So, she took a deep breath and waited for him to speak.

"What game is this you're playing, Sara? Are you now using your favors to try to get what you want? Is that it?" He towered over her in reproach.

Sara refused to shrink from him as she had at other times when he'd used this tactic. She stood tall and answered, "No, Geoff. I made love with you last night because I felt loving toward you, that's all. It had nothing to do — one way or the other — with continuing choir practice. I can find room in my heart and in my life for you and for my love of song."

Geoff snorted in disgust. "Well, I can't. There's only room in my heart for you, not for your singing. And if you insist on trying to make me accept this, I might not even find room in my heart, or in my life, for you at all anymore."

"Then I feel sorry for you, Geoff," Sara said quietly, "because that means your heart is very shallow. Don't you understand that the more love you give out, the more love you have to give? Can't you see that when you express the love you have inside you — like I do both by taking care of the family and by singing — the fuller your heart grows because it's like a river that flows in the shape of infinity and is without end? That when you love and give with all your heart, it always comes back to you multiplied?"

"And where did you get that nonsense? At church?" Geoff sneered. "I've given plenty of love in my life, and I've never seen it come back to me multiplied."

"Oh have you?" Sara challenged. "Or have you really only given out a childish plea for love, a one-sided, limited, conditional imitation of love that seeks what no one can fulfill because you won't let them, because you stifle them with your demands in your fear that you'll lose their love?"

Geoff reared back as if Sara had struck him. "I don't have to listen to this!" he said, reaching inside the door for the car keys that hung from the rack next to it.

"Okay, run away like you always do, Geoff. Just know, while you're out there doing damage to yourself and to us and to our family, that we do love you, despite it all. And we'll still be here when you get home."

"Oh will you, now?" Geoff scoffed, arching his eyebrows ridiculously as he shouldered himself into his car. "Or will you be off at choir practice again?"

"Just because I'm gone for a few hours every evening for a month or so, doesn't mean I'm not here for you, Geoff."

The slamming of the car door, the roaring of the engine, and the squealing of the tires as Geoff peeled out of the garage was all the response she got. But Sara refused to give in to the feeling of despair that threatened to overwhelm her. She'd placed her trust in the Almighty, and to give in would be to take that trust back. Something would happen to change Geoff's heart, she was certain of it.

Chapter 6

Just as Sara was leaving practice that night, feeling buoyed by the wonderful songs they'd sung—including a modern, soulful arrangement of "Amazing Grace" which was one of her all time favorite songs—her cell phone rang. "Hello?" she answered, her light heart growing heavy at the thought that it might be one of the children calling due to a problem with their father.

"Sara, it's Geoff. I'm at the police station."

"The police station!" Sara bit off a yelp of alarm and quickly lowered her voice on the last two words. "What are you doing at the police station, Geoff?" she hissed, heading swiftly out the door and down the walkway outside the church that led to the parking lot.

"I'm in jail."

Sara opened her car door and slid into the driver's seat, shutting the door hurriedly. The windows were up so she felt safe to raise her voice as she asked, "What are you in jail for, Geoff?"

"I got a D.U.I. I have to stay here at least 24 hours, maybe longer, until I get a hearing. I can't drive until I get a work only permit, so I'll need you to pick me up when they let me out." Geoff said it as though it was an inconsequential parking ticket he'd gotten, which instantly riled Sara.

"You did this on purpose, didn't you? You wanted to make sure I couldn't continue with the choir and the recording, so you went out and did this!" she accused.

"Are you nuts?" was his response. "You think I would willingly put my job in jeopardy, not to mention pay the stiff fines and fees and higher auto insurance they're going to slap me with just to stop you from singing?"

"Yes, yes I do. I think you'd go to any lengths to get what you want, no matter who you hurt—you've already proved that to me over the last fifteen years!" Sara was glad Geoff couldn't see her, couldn't see how violently she was trembling with a rage that bubbled up like molten lava from a volcano that had appeared to be dormant. "Well, it won't work, you hear me? I don't care if you have to ride a bike, walk or crawl to get where you need to go! I will not be your personal taxi, and I will not let you and the mess you've gotten yourself into keep me from making this recording, or from attending church and choir, even after the CD is finished. So find your own way home when they let you out, you got that?" she yelled and hit END on her cell phone.

Then she sat in her car for a good ten minutes trying to calm down so she wouldn't get a ticket herself for driving under the influence of a reckless fury. While she was at it, she yelled at God, too. "Is this Your answer to my faithful prayer? To put my husband in jail and cause the family extra financial stress and strain? What if Geoff loses his job over this? Don't You even care what will happen to the rest of us? And what kind of a holiday season will we have now? Gee, thanks, thanks a lot!"

Once she finally simmered down and grew quiet, Sara thought she could hear a voice that wasn't a voice, yet was stronger than any she'd ever heard, speaking to her, and the message it gave her was that everything happened for a reason. It assured her that even though the reason might be beyond her understanding, everything was working out as it should. It told her that her trust wasn't misplaced; only her heart. *"Take heart."* She felt the words deep within her own heart and a sense of peace that was indescribable came over her.

The late autumn night was misty and as the fog crept around the car, enclosing Sara in with it, she said, "I apologize. I was childish to act as I did, and to worry, of all things, about the upcoming holiday season, when it really is all about You; or it should be. Thank You for working in my life in ways I may not always understand but that I know are in answer to my faith in You. Even though that faith — my faith — wavered, I realize that Yours never does. Thank you.

Thank you. Thank you." Then, aware of the lateness of the hour and knowing she needed to get home to her children, Sara turned the key in the ignition and drove home in the murky darkness with care.

It was the first time that Sara had spent an entire night alone in their marriage bed in fifteen years. Yes, there were lots of nights that Geoff came home in the wee hours, and yes, Sara had spent many sleepless hours before this, but this time her insomnia was due to something else altogether. Unlike on other occasions, tonight she knew exactly where her husband was. For once her troubled thoughts weren't focused on him but on herself.

Because Geoff wasn't the only one who was at fault.

As Sara had tossed and turned, it came to her that she was almost as much to blame for Geoff's bad behavior as he was. By not standing up for herself, by allowing him to run roughshod over her feelings and ignore her needs, by giving in to his tantrums and doing all she could to pacify him, Sara had created a monster. And she'd done the same thing with the children, giving in to them, allowing them to treat her in the same way their father did so that they became mini monsters. Not only that, but she had enlisted their help in overly-cosseting their father, so that they, too, fed the beast otherwise known as Geoffrey Alan Avery.

It wasn't a pretty thing to acknowledge her own culpability. It was devastating to realize what she'd done to herself, to her children, and to Geoff. She tried to rationalize, to excuse herself. She hadn't meant to do anything wrong. She was only trying to keep peace, to be a good wife and mother in the only way she knew how. But the voice that wasn't a voice disagreed, and Sara cringed from it. She was forced to own up to being a closet martyr, someone who was filled with crippling self-pity and — worse — a raging resentment that no one appreciated all the sacrifices she had made for them. She had lain herself upon the altar of the false god of Pride, the secret pride that she had taken in being needed, and all she had done was make Geoff and the kids overly-dependent on her and nearly destroy the family. The pearl gray skies of dawn were visible through her bedroom windows before she finally stopped trying to defend her actions and accepted one hundred percent that the buck stopped with her.

Sara resolved that she would salvage what she could. The children were already showing signs of self-sufficiency and recovery, as was she, but Geoff...Geoff was still lost among the ruins. She admitted that she'd failed to do right by him, once again, when they'd had their altercation about the D.U.I. over the phone. Instead of showing her husband love, despite his carelessness, she'd hurled angry words and condemnation at him. That hadn't been necessary. She could have stuck to her guns without firing them on him. She'd never make what was wrong in their marriage right by adding yet another wrong to it.

When Geoff came home, she would apologize to him for accusing him of deliberately getting pulled over for drunk driving, and then they would have to talk. "Thank You for opening my eyes," Sara said, even as her lids were drooping, heavy with the need for sleep. "Thank You in advance for opening my husband's ears and heart."

Chapter 7

True to her resolve, Sara refused to pick Geoff up after his hearing two days later, on Thursday, and it wasn't to punish him, although he might not believe that. It was because she'd been enabling him under the guise of caring for him, and it was time to stop. Nor did she call his work on Wednesday, the day after the arrest, and make excuses for him, as she had done when he overindulged in the past. No, from now on, whatever Geoff did, Geoff would have to deal with. She would allow him to face the consequences of his own actions, and that also went for the kids. If he hadn't called his place of employment or couldn't get permission to call, that was his problem. She went to choir practice the next night, Wednesday, Teen Night, and took the children with her, as though her husband wasn't sitting in jail at all.

When Geoff got home Thursday afternoon around three-thirty, Sara, Abby and Aidan were already in the process of preparing an early dinner, lasagna again, since they hadn't gotten to enjoy the previous batch. Sara was leading the two of them in a rousing rendition of "Awesome God" — which had been chosen as a track for the upcoming CD — while she stirred the sauce that Abby had put together. Abby was carefully dumping cooked lasagna noodles into a colander in the sink, and Aidan was grating cheese. It hadn't felt this cheerful in their home in a very long time, but as soon as Geoff walked through the door, everyone halted what they were doing and waited with baited breath for him to come down on them.

But Geoff, whom Sara had expected would be more than usually irate, especially since she hadn't pandered to him and she hadn't yet had a chance to explain her reasons for not being there for him, surprised them all by asking, quite casually, "What's that song you were singing? Don't stop on my account. Please—keep going."

They looked at him askance, convinced that he was baiting some sort of trap for them. No one let out a peep.

"I'm not going to get mad, I promise," Geoff said. "I really do want to hear the rest of that song."

Giving him the benefit of the doubt—although she found his suddenly accepting attitude disquieting—Sara sang the next verse of the song. Abby and Aidan hesitantly joined in on the chorus, and then an amazing thing happened.

Geoff's bass voice accompanied them.

The kids looked at him like he'd grown two heads before they broke into such huge smiles they could hardly continue. The whole family sang the chorus over again to finish.

Then Geoff asked, "What can I do to help?" and Sara's jaw dropped open. She couldn't believe what was happening, wouldn't dare to believe it. Her husband couldn't have changed overnight, not after so many years of being a domineering boor. Still, a small seed of hope lodged itself deep in her heart at his unexpected overtures.

"Well sir," she told him with a small smile, "since we're doing the cooking and it's almost done and the table is already set, you can clear and wash the dishes after I leave for practice."

"Deal," he said without censure, flashing her the dimpled, lopsided grin that had made her fall in love with him in the first place. Sara nearly fainted. What in the world had happened to Geoff in the past 48 hours to make him act this way? Whatever it was, and even if it didn't last, she was going to enjoy it while she could.

Over the next three days, Geoff came home by six, not later. Of course, his restricted license could have something to do with it, but because he continued to show support to all of them — helping the kids with their homework, doing dishes, and even cooking a rudimentary skillet meal of scrambled eggs mixed with fried potatoes, onions and sausage for dinner one of the nights — Sara began to believe his heart had truly been changed.

That Saturday night, when Sara came home from practice and found no one downstairs, she climbed to the movie den upstairs, and there he was, sitting between the kids on the sofa, holding the big bowl of popcorn that they shared on his lap, watching *Avatar*, a favorite of both Abby and Aidan, with them. "Hi, I'm home," Sara said, gazing on the trio with an indulgent smile.

"Hi honey," Geoff replied with a smile. (That was another thing that had changed. Instead of saying she was a "sorry excuse for a wife" and other verbally abusive things, he now dropped endearments like they were candy and he was the piñata they spilled out of, calling her "sweetheart" and "sugar" and sprinkling little kisses on her cheeks, her lips, her forehead, the sensitive spot on the nape of her neck.) Now, he handed the bowl of popcorn to Abby and roused himself from the sofa to come over and put his arms around her. He nuzzled the side of her neck and whispered, "Can we go downstairs a minute? I need to talk to you privately."

"Eyew, Dad, get a room," Aidan said.

"Watch it, buster!" Geoff retorted in a mock-mean voice. He took Sara's hand. "Come on."

When they were well out of earshot of the kids, sitting on the overstuffed couch in the living room, he took both her hands in his and said, "I have something important to ask you. I'll understand if you say no, but I sincerely hope you won't." Geoff looked at her earnestly, and Sara felt his hands trembling. Was he nervous? What could he want that would cause him to act like he did on the day he first proposed?

"What is it, Geoff?" Sara smiled reassuringly at him, though she felt a flutter of anxiety in the pit of her stomach because of the way he was acting.

He rubbed the back of one of her hands with his thumb unconsciously and cleared his throat. "Would it be alright..." he stopped, hesitated, seemed uncomfortable.

"Would what be alright?" Sara prompted.

He hawked again, took a deep breath and squared his shoulders. "Would it be alright if I went to church with the rest of you tomorrow?"

Sara's eyes widened. She sat silent, unmoving, completely dumbfounded. Of all the things she envisioned him asking, she'd never in a million years have guessed he'd ask this.

Geoff took her silence for a negative answer. His face fell and he mumbled, "Never mind, that's okay," even though it clearly wasn't. "I can wait until you're ready to have me there."

"Oh, Geoff," Sara cried, "of course, I want you to join us! I've been waiting for this day ever since you stopped coming to church with me after we got married. But I just don't understand."

She asked the question that had been a constant refrain in her mind over the past several days, "What's happened to you?" She didn't give him time to answer and rushed to clarify, "Not that I mind, but this total turnaround of yours freaks me out. Honestly, I'm afraid to trust it."

"Well," Geoff said with a hangdog expression on his face, "I guess I can't blame you for that. I accused you of being a 'sorry excuse for a wife' but I'm the one who's been a sorry excuse for a husband, super sorry. So sorry, I don't deserve for you to believe how sorry I really am. But Sara, I am. I had my eyes opened the night I spent in jail, and I promise you, I'll never go back to being the jerk I was, not ever again." He pulled her left hand up and kissed her wedding ring, like she was a queen and he was her servant.

Shaking her head in wonder, Sara asked, "What opened your eyes, Geoff?" An unpleasant thought occurred to her and she tacked on, "No one did anything to you, did they?"

"Not unless you count totally changing my heart, no. No one did anything bad to me. You would have noticed the battle scars by now if they had even tried." He shook his head. "No, I just happened to meet a very special person in that jail cell, and after that person introduced me to myself I didn't like what I saw, not one little bit."

"So who was this person? I'd sure like to meet him," Sara smiled.

"I don't know his name. All I know is that he was thrown in the cell with me. He was all bruised and bloodied, like he'd been in a fight. When I asked him what happened, he said a bunch of teenage boys jumped him in a back alley, but that he had it coming to him…"

"How so?" Geoff asked the guy.

"Oh, I didn't have it coming from them. I didn't even know who they were. They were after my watch and my wallet. But I deserved every bit of the beating they gave me, believe me."

"What makes you think that, if you didn't even know them?"

"Well…" the man hung his head a moment, then raised it and looked Geoff straight in the eyes. A strange feeling passed through Geoff, something like a shiver of premonition, as he returned the man's steady gaze. "I am – was – a rotten person. All I ever thought about was myself. I went out and partied and chased skirts, and I treated my wife and kids like they were a bunch of old clothes I was tired of wearing. I was never there for them. That didn't stop me from putting them down for wanting to do anything other than be there for me, especially my wife. She was an artist – "

"Wait a minute, what do you mean 'was'?"Dread coursed down Geoff's spine. He didn't want to know where this was going, but yet he had to know.

"I'm getting to that," the man said, and his bright blue eyes darkened with sorrow. He scrubbed his hands over his face, and Geoff noticed that two of the fingers on his right hand were extremely swollen and disjointed. He should have been taken to the hospital.

"My sweet Cara was a fine artist, but I couldn't stand anyone in the family having the limelight other than me, so I belittled her sculptures — and her as a woman — every chance I got. When she turned away from me in the sack because I was drunk and reeking of another woman's perfume, I told her she was just as bad in bed as she was at sculpting. I said it was no wonder I sought comfort in another woman's arms."

His voice hitched, but he visibly forced himself to continue. "Oh, God, I'd give anything to take it all back — anything — but I can't. I started staying out more and more often, drinking more and more heavily, and my kids, oh, dear Lord, my kids, they had to listen to me and their mother fighting. One night, I was so drunk that it was a wonder I didn't get a D.U.I. When I got home, Cara was waiting up for me. She didn't say a word, just looked at me like she was a wounded deer and I'd shot her. I couldn't take that look, so I hit her, tried to wipe it off her face. When she screamed, the kids — I had twin seven-year-old boys — came running into the room, and they screamed when I hit her again, so I turned around and hit them, too. I'd never hit any of them in my life before, I swear — I hollered and carried on, but I never hit them. I did that night, though. Oh

God, that night..." The man stopped, overcome by wracking, gut-wrenching sobs.

Geoff's insides curdled as he listened, and he wanted to walk away from the terrible confession that could so easily have been his own, but there was nowhere to go. He was a prisoner of more than just the jailhouse. He was chained to this stranger by his own guilt.

After what seemed like an eternity, the guy pulled it together and said brokenly, "I killed them. I killed them all..."

Get me out of here! was Geoff's silent response. I'm trapped in this cell with a murderer. Get me out!

"If you killed them, then why are you here instead of in prison?" Geoff blurted out his next thought. "Unless you just now did what you're saying you did?"

"No, no jury will convict me, but I killed them just the same. After I whaled on all of them, I took off again, left them all crying, headed for an all night liquor store and finished the drunk I started. I passed out in my car in the parking lot of the store. When I woke up the next afternoon, I felt horrible, and not just because of the hangover. For the first time in my life, I wanted to apologize, to make it up to them. I knew I'd gone too far.

"I went to a toy store and bought my boys the scooters they'd been hounding me for, and then I hit a florist's and bought my wife a dozen red roses. But when I got home, there was nothing there but a burned-out shell..."

"Your house burned down? How did that happen? Was the

family alright?" Geoff couldn't help but voice the questions even though he really didn't want to hear the answers.

The man started shaking so hard, Geoff thought he might be having the DTs, so he got up, went to the intercom, started to press the button to call for assistance, but the man shook his head as he held up a hand and said, "I'm alright."

Geoff sat back down on his bunk. The guy shook his head again and said, "No. No, that's not true. I'll never be 'alright' again, but I'm physically okay, even though I wish I wasn't. I wish it was me that was dead. I wish I could give up my life for theirs, make a swap, but it doesn't work that way.

"When I went to the fire department," he continued in a hollow voice, "the fire chief told me that there were three victims of the fire, and that they hadn't been able to contact me, even though the neighbors gave them my cell number. I turned it off before I went on my binge. He said that there would be an investigation into the cause, but all he could tell me at that moment was that the bodies were burned beyond recognition but he assumed they were my wife and children, and that the fire had been so intense virtually no effects were left among the rubble. He said there was some speculation that a propane tank explosion caused the fire, but they wouldn't be certain of that until they got the results of the investigation.

"I knew, though, the instant that he mentioned the propane tank, that it was my fault. I'd backed into something in the garage as I was leaving that night, but I didn't stop to see what I'd hit as I

peeled rubber out of there. I'd forgotten all about the spare propane tank for the grill that was sitting in the garage. When I hit it, I must have punctured it. Most likely Cara closed the garage door after me, and then as soon as the electronic igniter on the gas hot water heater that was also out there in the garage kicked in — ka-boom! There went my entire life, up in flames."

"Oh, man, I'm sorry," Geoff said. He didn't know what else to say. But he did know, as he spoke the words, that he needed to say them, and mean them, to someone other than this shell of a person who sat next to him. "So, if it wasn't your fault, why are you in here now?"

"But it WAS my fault!" the man sobbed. "It was my fault."

"Okay, so it was your fault, but that's not why you're in here now, is it?" Geoff reworded his question, hoping that would get a response.

But he never did get the answer he sought. All the man said, over and over, for the rest of the night was, "Cara, oh Cara! I'm in here because I deserve to be in here. I deserve to be locked up forever. I deserve to get the chair, I deserve to be shot. Cara, my sweet Cara! I'm in here because I deserve to be in here…"

"When he kept calling for his wife, Cara, all I could hear in my head was 'Sara'. It almost made me go as insane as he was. I was never so glad to see morning come as I was that day. I couldn't wait to come home and tell you how much I loved you, but then you refused — and rightly so — to come and pick me up, and I knew I'd have my work cut out trying to earn your forgiveness. I owe that man, big time, for making me realize what I truly have, and I don't want to lose you — or the kids." Geoff's eyes filled with tears. "Can you forgive me, my beautiful, precious, songbird Sara?"

Sara looked at the man who'd by turns brought her so much joy, then so much misery. A mean little part of her wanted to punish him for awhile by withholding from him the absolution he sought. But, somehow, all the bad things he'd said and done over the years just melted away in the fiery intensity of his loving gaze, and all she could remember now were the good times.

"Oh, I don't know," she said sliding her gaze away from his. She could feel him tensing up in the way he tightened his grip on her hands. Then she looked back at him and in her eyes there was an echo of the love in his. "It might just take me a lifetime to get over it completely." Her lips twitched with the urge to giggle, and Geoff saw them. He leaned over and sucked the giggle out of her with his kiss.

Chapter 8

The next month flew past in a blur. Sara honed her talent for singing as the choir prepared to cut the CD, and Geoff discovered a long-buried talent of his own — that of being a family man. He developed this talent by coming home early from work whenever possible and pitching in on most of the nights Sara was at practice, except when she dropped him off at A.A. meetings beforehand. Sometimes, this talent was rusty — he didn't always say or do the right thing, and Abby and Aidan were quick to let him know it; often, he burned what was his to learn to cook; and his housekeeping skills were deplorable — he did things like washing reds with whites so they came out pink; forgetting to add dishwasher detergent to the dishwasher so that dishes didn't come clean and had to be run through a second cycle; and adding too much soap to the washer so that the laundry room was swamped in bubbles (that one turned out to be a lot of fun for him and the kids since they held a bubble creation contest and topped it off with a bubble battle, then hurriedly sopped up the mess using nearly every towel in the house before Sara came home) — but he was sincere in his efforts, so they all forgave him; after all, no one became a Michelangelo overnight. Geoff was especially caring of Sara when she came home from practice, bringing her hot cocoa, pushing the ottoman under her tired feet and massaging those same feet, surprising her with little love notes, and showing her in other ways how much he cherished her. The household bloomed under all this extra attention, and Geoff, the unexpected gardener, had a new twinkle in his eyes, despite the mess he'd created financially when he got the D.U. I.

His manager at the company where he worked didn't fire him, and Geoff was aware he'd been extremely blessed by that. Because he'd been such an asset to them up until he didn't show or call in for work those few days, Mark Dunham only docked him some vacation days to make up for the time they'd been without his services. They had a long "heart talk" in which Geoff was completely honest about what had happened and how he intended to make amends.

"I can't be your party boy, anymore, Mark," he told his boss. "I'm on the verge of becoming a full-blown alcoholic, and that's not what I want for my life. I've left my family to manage on their own for the past fifteen years. I was about to lose them before I got the D.U. I. and someone I met in jail turned my head around. I've neglected them for far too long. I need to be there nights and weekends for them from now on. I'm also mandated by the court to attend A.A. meetings."

"I understand, Geoff, believe me. Just between you and me, I've already lost my family, and I wish I'd been brave enough to take the same stand with the CEO that you just did with me. If you don't mind not claiming all the credit for your work, I'll let Thom Taylor—he's young and hungry, and single—schmooze our clients from here on out."

"The only thing that worries me about that is the guy could end up with my job," Geoff said, his brows drawing together in a frown. Then something spoke to him from deep inside, and almost instantly, his forehead smoothed out. He added, "But that's the chance I'll have to take if I want to keep my family intact, isn't it?" He was learning to trust in a Power higher than himself, and whatever happened would be what needed to happen, of that he was certain.

Now Geoff went with the family to church every Wednesday evening and found himself roped into assisting with Teen Night, something he enjoyed much more than he ever thought he would because that little boy inside him who never quite grew up could have carte blanche here, so long as he didn't throw one of his tantrums. Oh, the old Geoff was still there—and he still did throw fits every now and then—like when he screwed something up at home—but the fits were of shorter duration, much less violent, and getting further and further apart the more he surrendered to the loving Presence within.

* * *

That Christmas in the Avery household was especially joyful, even though there wasn't a lot of money for gifts. In fact, they drew names and each person bought one gift and one gift only for the name they drew. Despite the sparseness of packages under the tree, there was much warmth in the house. A roaring fire crackled in the hearth of the living room fireplace; the aroma of roasting turkey wafted in from the kitchen; the tree was adorned with glowing white lights and multitudes of angels—Sara's secret collection of ornaments finally brought out of hiding—and there were huge smiles on every face as the stereo played and everyone sang along, filling the room with the sounds of their enthusiastic, if not especially adept, accompaniments to Sara, the songbird, whose voice soared above theirs in the room—and on the newly-released CD. Her personal life was now a testament to the miracle of the healing power of love, her long buried talent uncovered and redeemed for the Master at last.

St. Matthew 25:15 ~ "And unto one he gave five talents, to another two, and to another one; to every man according to his ability…"

St. Matthew 25:18 ~ "But he that had received one went and digged in the earth, and hid his lord's money…"

A Special Message from the Author

Dear Reader,

This was what I originally wrote when I gave away my bestselling inspirational short story, *Jesus on a Park Bench*, on Kindle for five days beginning on the initial publication date below:

12-24-12

Dear Reader,

These are tough economic times for us all. And I realize that, for some of us, the festivities of Christmas only serve to bring our suffering more sharply into focus. But I would challenge each and every one of you to step outside yourselves and do something for someone less fortunate this holiday season, even if it's only to talk with them and acknowledge them as fellow human beings. You will be uplifted by it, I guarantee you. "J." told me so.

May you be blessed by the reading of this little story, my gift to you.

Merry Christmas with love,

Shari Broyer

Today, 1-10-14, as I prepare to put this new inspirational novella, *Buried Talents*, into publication via CreateSpace and

Kindle, I would like to add this note, which I have already sent out to friends and family:

Taking *Jesus on a Park Bench* "To the Streets"

If you've received an email from me asking for your help, it's because I've been led by Spirit to take the little e-book that I wrote and give it to the homeless at Christmas, 2013. That wee story, which I only really intended to give to family and friends as the only gift I had to give, took off and still remains in the top 100 of the inspirational category even now, over a year later, moving onward toward its third Christmas season. It has struck a chord with thousands of readers.

I'll be completely honest and say that the woman in the story was me, fictionalized. At Christmas of 2012, I was really down, financially and emotionally. I'd lost a couple of good friends of many years; I was about to be hired for a seasonal income tax position but hadn't yet started the job and all my money was gone; and my son, whom I dearly love, had stopped contacting me. I couldn't see the good that still remained—all I could see was that I was on the brink of homelessness, and I was all alone. So, as I've done many times in my life when faced with hardship, I started writing. What came out of me not only made me feel better, I've discovered it has encouraged many other people and helped them to better appreciate what they have, as well. One man contacted me privately to say he was going to use the story to help him through some hard times, and several Amazon reviewers have said they value what they have more because of the "reminder" my story has been to them.

I've been ashamed to admit that my son is a drug addict who has basically lived on the streets since he left home at eighteen. Pride has no place in what I'm attempting to do, so I'm humbling myself to tell you this. I've taken him in many, many times and tried to help him, but it's always come down to him or me. I've had to learn self-preservation and force myself to stick to my boundaries. My son is thirty-three now, and it's been so hard to watch him on his downward spiral and be helpless to do anything. I've felt like a failure as a mother more times than I can begin to count, but I know that my son is the one who must find redemption for himself. My son is loving, kind, helpful and very smart, but he can't see the good in himself anymore. (Jay, in the story, is not only molded on the great Master, Jesus Christ, but also on the good at the core of my son's heart).

I have begun praying: "Thank You, God, for healing my son. Thank You for sending him back to me. Thank You for making him an instrument of Your Divine will." I do believe that there is a future for my son in helping others get clean once he is free of his addictions. I feel it deeply within my soul. I don't know when that day will come, but I have faith *it will come*. I ask that everyone who reads this please pray the same faith-filled prayer I do for my son's healing.

I'm not sure if the project I've already embarked upon will help him personally, although I gave him one of the first POD copies of ***Jesus on a Park Bench*** when I made a trip to CA and found him back in August of 2013. We talked, cried and hugged, and he read ***Jesus on a Park Bench*** with me and kept it. I have to believe the message it contains — "now there is everything to gain" — will penetrate when it is supposed to and do what it is meant to do.

On December 23, 2013, my first Christmas giveaway to the homeless was made possible by my fund-raising efforts (word of mouth, giving copies of my book to secure donations, and receiving monetary donations from patrons at a local library). I gave out 150 copies of my little book with $5 gift certificates for McDonald's at The Henry Unger Kitchen, under the auspices of Saint Vincent DePaul Catholic Church, which feeds around 1300 homeless per day. Most come from the Central Arizona Shelter Services next door in downtown Phoenix.

I raised a total of over $1,700 for the books and gift cards, and one woman donated 55 hand-crocheted hats for me to give to the homeless, too. It was an amazing experience which

I've blogged about under the tab "**To the Streets**" on my website **http://sharibroyerbooks.weebly.com**.

I want to continue with the project and raise enough to reach ALL the homeless at that venue for Christmas 2014 (many were turned away), then add more legs (take it further abroad and add more services in the years to come). I have a lot of work ahead of me to pull this off, and I'm just in the beginning stages, but it's been laid upon my heart—and not just because of my son—to do this. If even one person in the homeless situation takes courage enough to pull themselves out of it through the message in *Jesus on a Park Bench*, then I feel my efforts will have been worth it.

So, what can you do to help? Please visit my website:

http://sharibroyerbooks.weebly.com

for specifics. Click on the "**To the Streets**" tab and read the blog entitled *How You Can Help*.

And please do reviews on Amazon of any of my books you read, especially *Jesus on a Park Bench*.

May hardened hearts be softened everywhere, so that one day, we may see the end of hunger, homelessness, and poverty.

Blessings to us all,

Shari Broyer

About the Author

Shari Broyer has been writing since she was first able to wield a pencil. Her earliest awards were a 1st place trophy for Creative Writing and certificate for First Runner-Up in Poetry at 8th grade graduation.

Formerly she was:

- Editor in Chief of Kent State University's Ashtabula campus literary magazine, *Kaleidoscope*
- Facilitator, Writers' Forum, Barnes and Noble, High Point, NC
- Host of *Writer's Digest* World's Largest Writing Workshop, Barnes and Noble, High Point, NC
- Published in various literary anthologies (most recently her poem "One-Eyed Jack" and "Squirrel" photo were featured in *Wild Edges — Manzanita, Poetry and Prose of the Mother Lode and Sierra*, released August, 2010)
- Top 100 winner, *Writer's Digest* 2000 competition — Inspirational category, *Shades of Gray*
- Winner of author Terri Weeding's Little Ole Humor Contest, etc.

She has been indie publishing her works for the past three years.

Shari does not like to be tied to a particular genre. She writes whatever her nine plus muses dictate. She is Spiritual, not of any one faith; instead she believes in and attempts to live according to the teachings of Jesus Christ.

Currently, Shari resides in Mesa, AZ and facilitates Writers Roundtable at Changing Hands Bookstore in Tempe, AZ. She is a member of American Christian Fiction Writers and its local Christian Writers of the West Chapter; Board Member/Newsletter Editor of the Desert Rose Chapter of Romance Writers of America, , and she is also a manuscript editor for hire. She welcomes your feedback at **shariannegaylee@gmail.com**, and invites you to visit her website, **http://sharibroyerbooks.weebly.com**.

27688813R00052

Made in the USA
Charleston, SC
18 March 2014